E
C6929m

STERLING, VIRGINIA
CHEROKEE STATE COLLEGE
CHEROKEE, N.C. 28719

My Darling Kitten

PETER COLLINGTON

Alfred A. Knopf   New York

RETA E. KING LIBRARY
CHADRON STATE COLLEGE
CHADRON, NE 69337

For Bon

E
C6929m

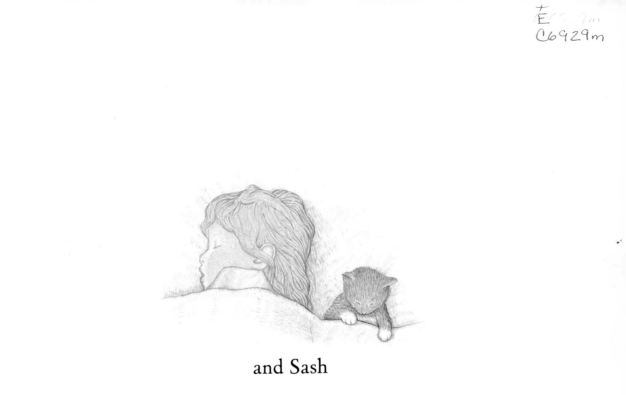

and Sash

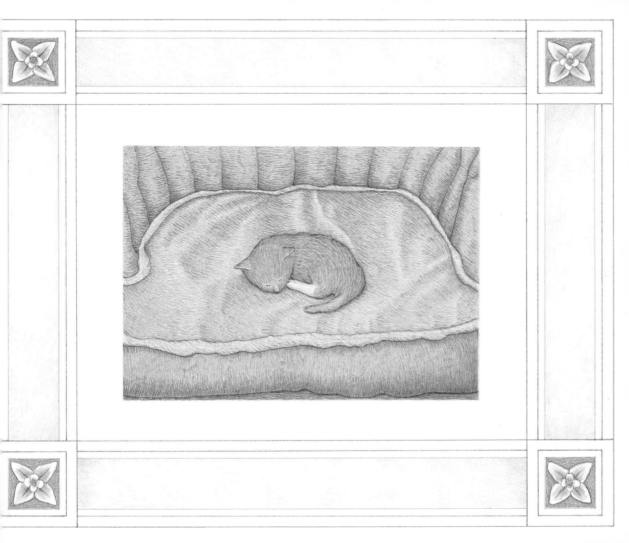

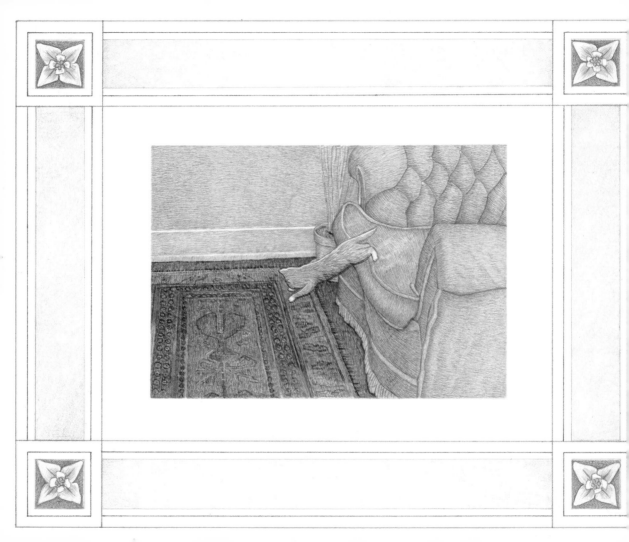

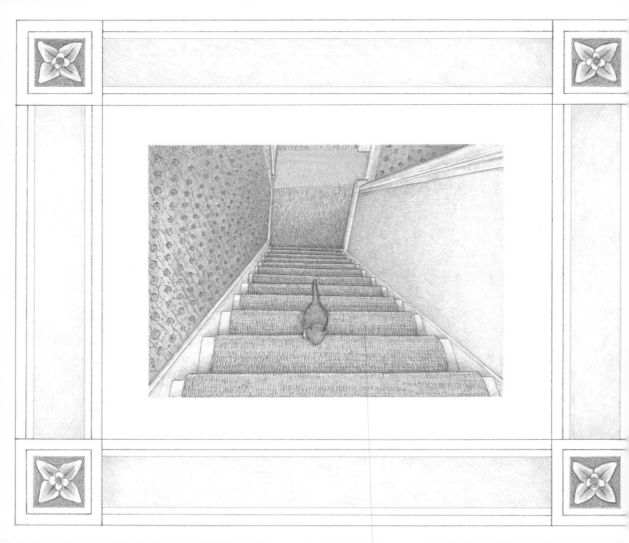

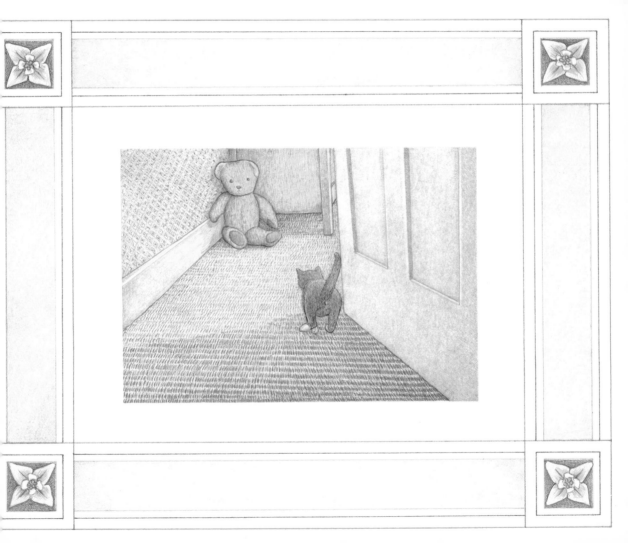

RETA E. KING LIBRARY
CHADRON STATE COLLEGE
CHADRON, NE 69337

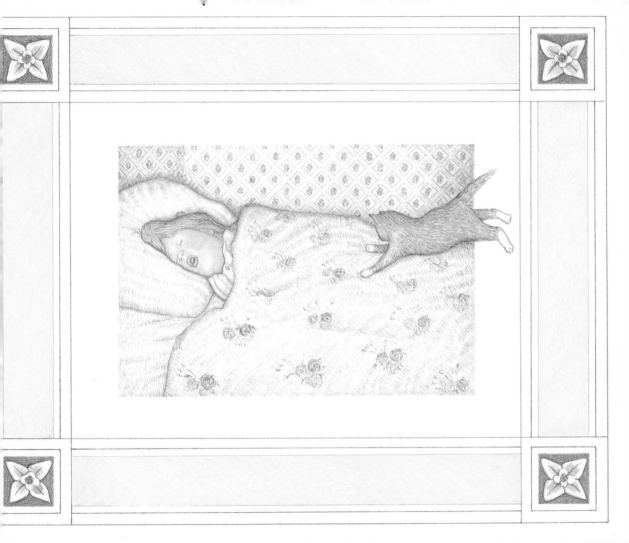

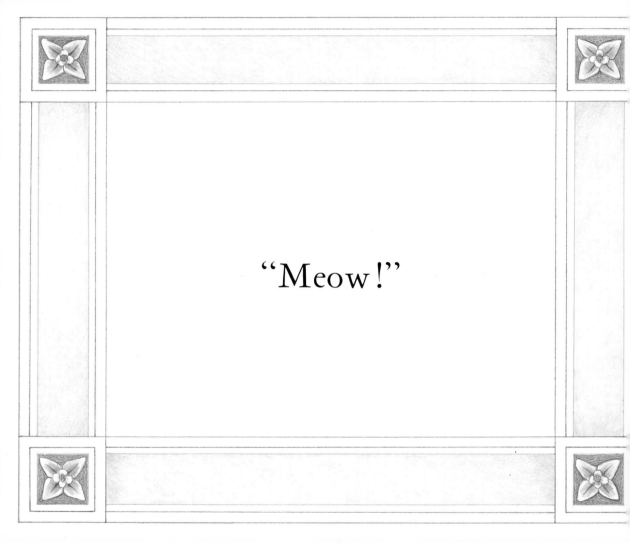

"Meow!"

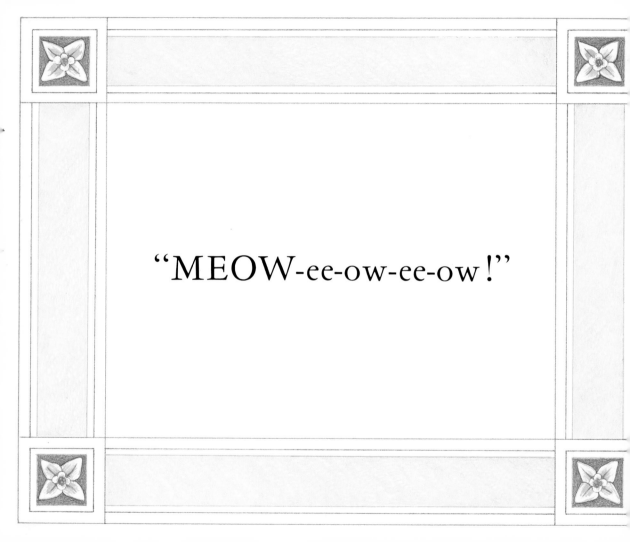

"MEOW-ee-ow-ee-ow!"

"My darling kitten!"

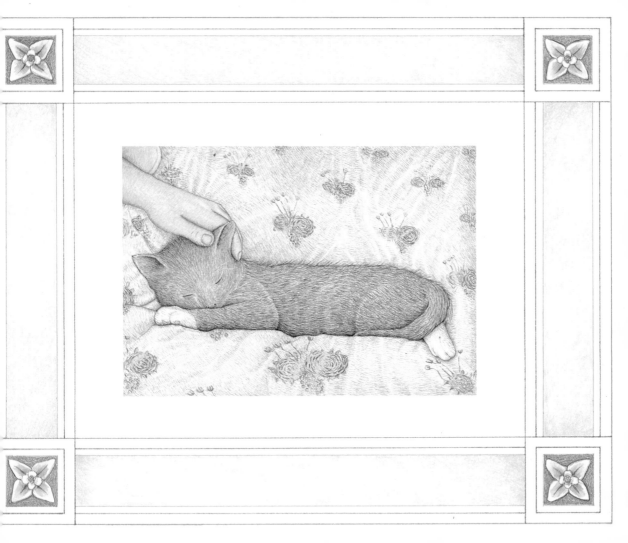

The End

This is a Borzoi Book published by Alfred A. Knopf, Inc.

Copyright © 1988 by Peter Collington

All rights reserved under International and Pan-American Copyright
Conventions. Published in the United States by Alfred A. Knopf, Inc.,
New York. Distributed by Random House, Inc., New York. Published in Great Britain by Methuen Children's Books Ltd., London.

Manufactured in Hong Kong by South China Printing Co.

2   4   6   8   10   9   7   5   3   1

Library of Congress Cataloging in Publication Data

Collington, Peter. My darling kitten / Collington Peter. p.   cm. Summary: After waking itself up, a kitten goes to wake up its sleeping owner.

ISBN 0-394-89924-5

[1. Cats—Fiction.]   I. Title.   PZ7.C686Dar   1988   [E]—dc19   87-31002